First published in Great Britain 1987 by Blackie and Son Ltd.

British Library Cataloguing in Publication Data

Cartwright, Stephen
My party.—(Blackie first storybooks)
I. Title
823'.914 [J] PZ7

ISBN 0-216-92197-X

Blackie and Son Ltd.
7 Leicester Place,
London WC2H 7BP

Printed in Singapore

My Party

Illustrated by Stephen Cartwright
Written by Jean Kenward

Blackie

It is my birthday. I am two.
I can dress myself.

Mummy and Daddy give me a birthday card.
I can open my birthday card.

I am having a party.

Mummy carries a table outside. ‘We can have the party in the garden,’ she says.

Mummy brings out plates and cups.
I put them on the table.

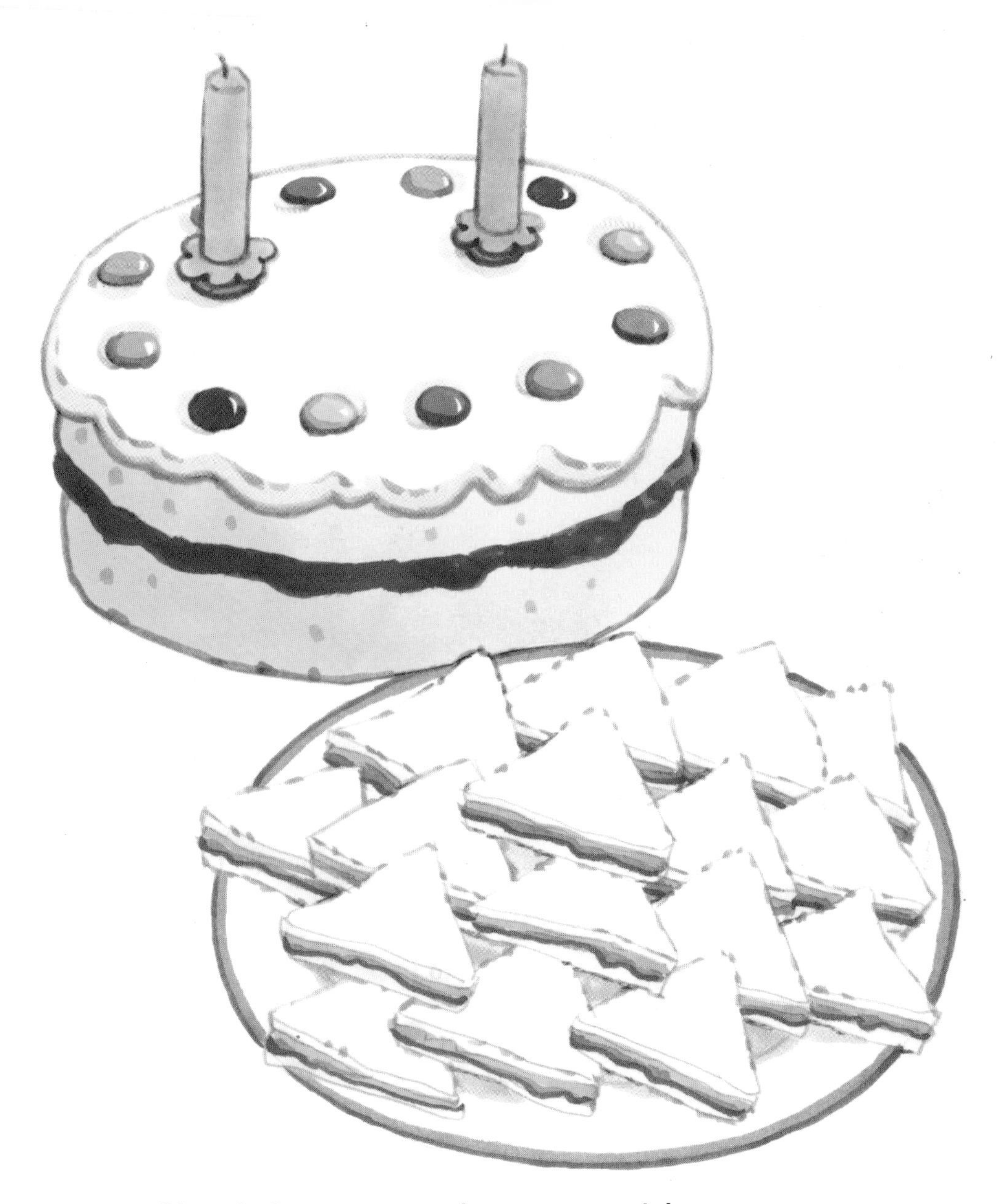

She brings out cheese and ham
sandwiches—and a cake!

Daddy ties some balloons on the front door.
Everyone can see it is my birthday.

All my friends arrive. They have presents for me! Their mums and dads go away, and leave them behind.

We have a treasure hunt in the garden.
Can you see the treasure?

It is hidden under a flower pot. It is a rubber duck.

We all sit down and get ready to eat.
I am feeling very hungry.

Suddenly a black cloud covers the sun.
It begins to rain hard!

'Carry all the food inside!'
cries Mummy.

We all run, carrying plates with us.
My friend, Sally, falls over.

We eat our food in the kitchen, in the living room, under the table, in the hall, in the bathroom, and on the stairs.

There are crumbs everywhere.
It is a great party. I like being two!